Anno Domini

Anno Domini

George Barker

faber and faber

First published in 1983
by Faber and Faber Limited
3 Queen Square London WC1N 3AU
Typeset by Wyvern Typesetting Ltd, Bristol
Printed in Great Britain by
Whitstable Litho Ltd, Whitstable, Kent
All rights reserved

© George Barker, 1983

British Library Cataloguing in Publication Data

Barker, George, *1913–*
Anno Domini.
I. Title
821′912   PR6003.A68
ISBN 0–571–13026–7

Library of Congress Cataloging in Publication Data

Barker, George, 1913–
Anno domini.

I. Title.
PR6003.A68A8   1983   821′912   82–25160
ISBN 0–571–13026–7 (pbk.)

To my wife

Contents

Acknowledgements

I wish to thank the Royal Literary Fund, without whose generosity these poems could not have been completed. I should also express my indebtedness to Mr Clive Sinclair, Mr John Cumming and Mr Hedley Marten.

Anno Domini

at a time of bankers
        to exercise a little charity;
at a time of soldiers
        to cultivate small gardens;
at a time of categorical imperatives
        to guess about clouds;
at a time of politicians
        to trust only to children and demigods.
And from those who occupy seats of power
        to turn, today, away
without incurring permanent reprisals.
        When the instruments of torture
are paraded in public places
        permit us to transmute them,
somehow, into ploughshares.
        When the tribulations of some tribes, or persons,
seem, as so often, to exceed a reasonable allotment,
        condescend, superior, to examine fate
and make sure that its machinery has not gone wrong.
        When those who deserve little more than
a severe whipping, wake up to a morning of pink
        champagne and strawberries,
visit them, surely, with one moment of retribution
        and slight indigestion. Expunge
from the punishment book of the frivolous
        those impositions incurred for singing at funerals;
and to the hopelessly optimistic
        award, if you will, a few kisses. When diagrams
dictate to our sympathetic systems, and the operation
        of stars deludes us that
it is wholly inauspicious,
        cheer us then, O Leda, with a kind
and silent light. Lord of the raddled and the penurious
        impute to those who have failed
no more serious an error than that of
        caring too much about success;

promote those who sit patiently twiddling
       their thumbs on benches, and let
even those who love Persian cats see, sometimes,
       that dogs are ours also.
Pardon if you will the thief or orphan or me
       stealing a meal from Babylon,
and the prince who absconds with the funds
       for a better reason. And let not,
let not everything we do
       become a final farewell.
Magister, legislate for us when on your
       circuit even we the guilty smirk in
our knowledge that greed motivates also
       the Grand Inquisitor with his bouquet of
feudal flowers, let alone the invidious
       putative I.
Supplant those who grow old with those who
       only grow roses, and let the Spanish
sun jockey all Black Princes back again into
       Aquitainian towers. Where dust storms prevail
let your face, Moses, appear on the mirage
       of Lebanon, speaking the one and
only word we can hear. Not by trial and error
       delegate to us those sorrows that rise from
our own trials and errors
       but dispose the Russian snows kindly towards us
so that they fall as warm as
       astra can. When on our tigers we
ride into Afghanistan
       loud with bullroarers,
call to our mind the fate of that Limerick girl
       who rode a tiger from Niger
but only one way. After those thunderstorms visit us
       in your most tender of forms,
the sky serene. And after eleven plagues
       as the white nurse come among the

seven sleeping survivors, and after all wars
         for a day withdraw from us
for only then may we see
         what it is we have done.
Strike the lamb dumb
         if it should Ego sing
and poleaxe the bull
         if it should bully the lamb
or bugger the powerless. When
         the knife of kisses excoriates
the flesh that it loves the best
         let the knife and lover be forgiven
and even perhaps the flesh.
         Hide, if you must, your face
from the homicidal maniac
         so that, though blind, he sees
you are not gone, but only
         like the moon turned away
from the crime which we cannot
         as yet understand, but must,
blind mystery of justice,
         believe to be somehow involved
in the exonerating epicycles of your will.

Will you also withdraw from those who
         carrying placards declaring
their total devotion to
         your service, proceed to demand
the death of their friends and even
         your enemies? Remove from
the crawling infant that instrument
         neither Heisenberg nor
Max Planck would ever dream
         of introducing into

a nursery, that little
                planetary construction of coloured
balls that seems likely to
                serve as our one and only
commemorative memorial? Among stars
                do I hear you whisper outside
their laboratories that yours yes
                yours was the first
but not the last big bang?
                For have you not, least hostile
of all possible hosts,
                amply provided us with
so much provender that,
                given the rope, and the hope,
what could we do save eat
                that bit of bread, loop up
the hanging hope, and trust
                in the end that the rope
would bear us up? Not
                no, not the belief.
I believe the belief
                fell from the lectern as
we sat and listened.
                But we forgot the words
and mistook those notes
                that fell, for, perhaps, music
When the little ones walk in
                the old garden what godsend
will descend upon them? Flowers?
                Or, astronomer, am I in error
and will what falls on them crush
                these kids like the grinding mills
and enormous prisms that turn
                so slowly, the altering stones and
looming epicycles—
                will these descend upon them?

They will, for these are truly
            the huge masonry of
collapsing belief. And so arraign but not
            too mildly those who purvey
arid principles among us
            as though they proffered us flowers.
Better than any belief
            the hope that survives the death
of formal dogma. Then
            on the day of showers
we depart on prolonged picnics.
            So my beloved bare
your throat to me and watch
            Absalom flash with kisses:
then let the old vulture do
            its deadly best to sing
and the corybantic drunk
            see visions of a blue
Fra Angelican clarity.
            Turn your hand not away
from the wilfully unemployed
            because they employ the state
as not from those whom the state
            only too wilfully employs. Mitigate
the frenzy of the erotic system
            in the heart of those who outlive
their time; transmute the ferocity
            of the fanatic into
a purpose conscious of moral proportion;
            a little tenderly flagellate
the flagellators, and lead back to the way
            (are we not all him?) the crossed
roads of the pervert. When
            at chance moments clouds of
change seem to do nothing
            but darken the landscape in which

we necessarily labour
        let a little illumination
from inexplicable sources
          descend on Breughelian fields.
Will you, at times, momentarily
        modify the optics of providence
so that some of us may see
          what best to do next? As when
the sleeping statesman dreams of the colour red
        and yet awakens with roses in his hands?
What tree will you eventually permit
        the uneaten apple of Eve to grow again on?

Then to whom save the prince of darkness
        shall we sacrifice a thousand
electric light bulbs? To whom save Machiavelli immolate
        a generation of truthful computers?
When the moon shines a construction
        of crystal and white lies appears in the garden
to commemorate all assassinated facts
        and the whitewashed elephants of
social hypocrisy. To whom else, then,
        save our rather unsavoury selves
shall we sacrifice the self-agonizing god?
        At a time of saints to encourage counterfeiters.
At a time of millionaire soccer stars
        to knit gloves for starving golliwogs.
Correct, O director, in time the fugitive clock
        that ticks a little too fast into
the future because it is sick both of the present
        and the forfeited past. Alleviate
the conscience of the deaf piano tuner
        who knows he knows no way to recognize
the perfect note, and knows, therefore,
        all notes must be imperfect.

Upon bad-tempered and hardened argufiers play
                the sprinkling hosepipe of
the heavenly humour that
                gave us the aardvark and the ballooning
hippopotamus. Vary in municipal gardens
                those strict arrangements of flowers
that remind us of German philosophers.

Impeach all presidents who seek
                to preside over private persons, and favour
all vendors of black ice cream.
                From congenital enemies remove
their passports, hobnailed boots and
                birth certificates so
that they think they are
                for the time being two quite
congenial persons. Comfort the brood
                of nine puppies with no foreknowledge
of a dog's life and let the caterwauling
                of microphones not abash serenaders.
For who—was it you?—made bleed and weep
                the laws of arithmetic as they nailed out
humanitas limb by limb like Jewish crucifixions on
                the hackenkreutz? Will you answer me?
I will retreat to archipelagoes where
                responses to these cloudy questions stalk
up and down proudly like red-stockinged
                flamingoes, and in the air such a plucking
of stringed instruments that the shipwrecked
                philosopher thinks that he hears
the psalteries of spiritual vision.
                Accord, then, to the stone-deaf, somehow,
an interpretation of these dialogues
                with which rocks and stones and trees

and particularly water
        seek continually to answer us.
Will your hand hesitate before
        it locks the undertaker's casket
on the unrepentant old lag, or the couple who,
        having nicer things, as they feel, to do
arrive a bit late for their funeral?
        Extend, that is, if you will, latitude
to those who steal little things, like, on Sundays,
        an hour of love. And to Arcadia lead
those among us, who, sleeping alone in suburbia,
        dream of goatherds and that
far-off unfabled Korya of honey-tongued brandy
        and brown bell-hung young goats
whickering in morning mountains.
        When homeward we
turn from distant Argos, grant
        that one blade of Agamemnon's
golden fields may somehow
        still tick in our memory or
whisper of honour to an attentive
        tympanum. May all Mycenaean
mountains remind us that over
        the darkest of caves and crimes
as over the violent lives of violent men
        the great white clouds of summer, like
compassion may sometimes, sooner
        or later, pass in a silent
propitiation. The birds fly daily
        out of such places as though
they brought from the haunts of the ruined
        ages news that the dead and the deserving
still dream in their famous tombs
        undisturbed by recurring
nightmares of the demi-urge,
        American engineers or the money spider.

As, over that ossified structure of
            intellectual dogma, the ziggurat
of scientific conviction,
            (the dogma that fact is
final, when we know it in truth
            to be no more than one story
of the Babbling Tower we
            astrologize in) over that
Manhattan of the mind let a sunrise
            or a shepherding sunset play
its many colours until
            all actual knowledge looks
like what it seems to be:
            a kaleidoscope inside
a magic lantern. For are there not
            always other shores and other
further marvellous islands
            where invisible flora
and fauna perform in their
            long-hidden gardens, where Lilith
may well awaken one brilliant morning
            again? Where are you leading me?
To that railway station, over-
            grown with fireweed, long-abandoned,
derelict, the signals dislocated,
            the sleepers uprooted, the name
by time erased, and the lines rusting
            after red rain? The station
without a crossing, where the mind, alighting,
            finds that it has arrived
in a place that exists alas
            no longer. Where the announcements
hang heavy with dead ideas,
            and consolations of the exhausted
conscience rot in flowerbeds
            like last year's roses.

In a time of fashionable evangelists
            to retire to small vegetable allotments;
in a time of doctors and aristocratic actresses
            to eavesdrop on the dialogues of worms;
in a time of national anthems and brass bands
            to conduct rigorous callisthenics for corpses;
in a time of bald-headed administrators
            to erect beribboned maypoles and
encourage cardsharpers; in a time of Scandinavian
            architecture and pornography to wrestle
with incubi and succubi; in a time of magicians and water
                                                                diviners
            to remember, nevertheless, that we can fly.
From moralistic and political trials
            allow us O lord chief justice to draw
our own biased conclusions without
            fear of the bell the book or the final
abomination. Persecute the persecutors, counsel the
                                                                counsellors
            and police the police:
Arraign the arraigners, mock the mockers and reform
            the reformers. Among
the shenanigans of moral foxes, O MFH,
            release the hounds of Here and Hereafter.
Modify the laws of cause and effect
            so that not even those guilty
of failed practical jokes like the Jesuits
            spend too long a time in Coventry.
Will you award a candle to those who whistle
            in valium dark? To those going under
for the third time, the lame, the dumb
            and any one else whom Seneca
might have thought monstrous,
            to them cast a rope or the branch
of a holly tree. Help us
            avoid a void. Nor let the moral philosopher

24

me numbers' *perpetuum mobile* or
that diastole and systole at
 art of things, the quixotic quanta, or
the principle that seeks to teach us
 e intellectual humility,
the will-o'-the-wisp perversity of
 ide-and-seek neutrino. It is then that
though very darkly we might see
 your wish or your will may be:
that, no less than
 nadman killing or shark with a red jaw
or the assassination of photographs or
 avalanche collapsing over
Obermann villages or the entire
 erse trying to find out
how wide it is, so we obey your will
 n we obey your image.
And tremble, then, at the mystery of evil.
 who will lay upon the stone
of the run-over child a wreath
 cribed: *Dei voluntas*. I will not, for there is a mystery here
not given to any, yet, to understand
 e printed shadows of Hiroshima, do they
point their evaporated hands at us
 you? How could it have been you?
This is a thing so evil that
 could have come from nowhere save a mind
capable of inventing the idea of evil.
 e are, professor, out of joint with the purpose
of your work; whatever that point may be,
 e are out of joint with it. You know.
Newman knew. We know. "The human race
 implicated in some aboriginal
calamity." This is the mystery, this
 alamity that, snakes coiled in its cloudy hair,
sits on the great tripod of past, present

drive us with whips into the practice of
moral philosophy, nor the humanitarian
with a discipline drive us into venal
love of one another, but mitigate
the myopia we suffer from whenever
we seek to perceive the working
of your gardener William in
the common or garden. On the
day when you speak shall I not hear but see?
In a time of vipers I will show
my sign. But if I walk down a street
in which I see no one else at all
but hear the footsteps and feel the presence
of a second person walking behind me,
shall I say, nevertheless, that I am alone,
or shall I confess that
I am subject to hallucinations?
What is the logic, Aquinas,
of this confusing image? All that I
think I perceive is rational and
conditioned by laws of
responsibility and reason: this,
in the simple sense, is reality. But those
footsteps persist and that presence
continues to follow or to precede me.

The Pyrrhic victories of the rational
surround us on all sides with
scenes of violence, carnage and
barbaric triumphal arches:
but somewhere in the mirage-ridden
hinterland of the spirit,
among the hallucinations and delusions
of that desert (which some of us

happily believe does not exist at all),
    somewhere there the crucifixion
of Adam is continually committed. I am that I am
    nailed up anew daily.
What are you looking for in this degraded
    landscape? Not for what is so
mysteriously there: for you are looking for
    what you have lost there
what you have done and won there
    but you are no longer looking for
what is and was and always will be so
    everlastingly there:
a dead-drunk conscience weeping
    over the mad and ravished Psyche.

In a time of hypochondriacal philosophers
    children play happily in public gardens;
in a time of statistics
    anarchy denudes herself of the seventh veil;
and in a time of magistrates
    criminals invent new crimes;
in a time of hedonists and belly dancers
    wise men draw the blinds and bolt the doors.
In a time of journalists most decent things
    acquire the gift of invisibility;
in a time of death all of us suddenly
    and miraculously discover that we are alive.
Sometimes favour, if you will, the arrogant
    of intellect with an odour as of
unknowable roses, and the proud man
    with a pair of unreliable braces.
Upon autumn lakes scatter the feathers
    of foolish patriots in foreign fields,
and bring to the beds of those who suffer
    a benign sister with a handful of poppies

not for remembrance, but to forget.
    As to Arcadia also
I bring that overloaded old bag of the eg
    covered with coloured stickers
enumerating the travelogue of vanity and
    expensive guilt, to find
that forgotten poppy also
    growing among those mountain
that still hide the dithyrambical
    and deathless Pan.
But can I confide to you, mediator,
    the fear I fear I fear
faced with the sleight of hand you perform
    upon the ascending spheres and
upon every day and the common place?
    As when rain chooses to fall upon
fields that need it, or the insane sun
    declines the whim to fry us like or
or as the star-fished sea
    keeps to its beds and basins on
the classroom globe.
    These things can be seen, I know,
as subject to simple laws. And these are the
    I find myself facing with a kind of
For, as I see it, these natural laws
    comprise the only evidence I can pe
of a superior purpose working
    up through all things. Thus when th
tree falls in October wind (as no less
    the sparrow's feather) it falls because
it was ordained to fall not by the laws
    of Time or Newton, but by the will
that upon all things has imposed its natural
    and even supernatural purposes.
As in the recurring seven-veiled dance of
    physics and the conundrum

and what future, hypnotizing the dove
            with catastrophic images of the possible.
And so all the stories that little children play-act
            on their picnics or by winter firesides,
tales of the Polyphemi–Frankenstein monsters
            that waken up and eat us, this is what you
doctor have done. Here is the mad creature
            you have created. Have you built your own
murder into the marvellous faculties
            we use because we possess?
What does this shambling machine whisper
            as it crawls and stumbles among rocks and ruins,
its clockwork eyes clouded with self-hate, its
            terminals cancerous, wetware and wordwrite
alphanumeric, phonemed,
            automatic forks pick-
ing up isotopes, robotics utterly grouched,
            the reproductive generator hanging
down like an obsolete decoration, the
            anthropic spirit skinnered, the
enigma cybernized,
            the circuit of the nervous system worn
to a nexus of Freudian wires,
            what does this shambling machine whisper
when it encounters, down the dark path,
            halfway through a Black Forest, of
a midwinter midnight,
            the huge god riding on a dead white horse?
What, what does it whisper?
            "I am a man"?

Arbiter of dreams open my sleep-walking
            eye upon scenes I cannot recognize
when in the morning I wake among nightmares. Let me see
            some humane minds still uncorrupted, some

good men not angling for
              even bigger fishes and some
women not cultivating Chinese little fingernails
              and poisonous flower power,
some farmers not ashamed of the name George, some
              doctors prepared to prescribe for ailments
not amended by penicillin, some gardeners providing
              a herb we seem to have lost, the *herba sacra*;
some couples actually thinking of truly
              mutual pleasures; some children
playing games without guns and some priests
              practically praying. Some birds in nests
not for sale and at evening some edible browsers
              grazing at grass; some small kingdoms
not constructing sub-atomic megakills; some
              cities not gormandizing spaghetti junctions;
some gardens growing a little wild in
              southern seaside townships; some
African elephants in Africa;
              some sunrises to which we may awaken
without the mind clouded by those poisoned
              vapours that now hang over every
mushroom field. But "Complaint",
              said a holy man, "is sin." Those mists
of the morning slowly disperse as
              the light climbs higher; invalids eventually
throw off sheets and step out into
              everyday rituals; overgrown even
battlefields after a time. Through a window
              in the gutted mansion
a flowering bush sooner or later
              pushes its optimistic blossoms
and from haunted lives one day
              the ghouls have fled, leaving
the kitchen just habitable; in the waste land
              a gypsy family has set up a homestead,

30

drive us with whips into the practice of
        moral philosophy, nor the humanitarian
with a discipline drive us into venal .
        love of one another, but mitigate
the myopia we suffer from whenever
        we seek to perceive the working
of your gardener William in
        the common or garden. On the
day when you speak shall I not hear but see?
        In a time of vipers I will show
my sign. But if I walk down a street
        in which I see no one else at all
but hear the footsteps and feel the presence
        of a second person walking behind me,
shall I say, nevertheless, that I am alone,
        or shall I confess that
I am subject to hallucinations?
        What is the logic, Aquinas,
of this confusing image? All that I
        think I perceive is rational and
conditioned by laws of
        responsibility and reason: this,
in the simple sense, is reality. But those
        footsteps persist and that presence
continues to follow or to precede me.

The Pyrrhic victories of the rational
        surround us on all sides with
scenes of violence, carnage and
        barbaric triumphal arches:
but somewhere in the mirage-ridden
        hinterland of the spirit,
among the hallucinations and delusions
        of that desert (which some of us

25

happily believe does not exist at all),
           somewhere there the crucifixion
of Adam is continually committed. I am that I am
           nailed up anew daily.
What are you looking for in this degraded
           landscape? Not for what is so
mysteriously there: for you are looking for
           what you have lost there
what you have done and won there
           but you are no longer looking for
what is and was and always will be so
           everlastingly there:
a dead-drunk conscience weeping
           over the mad and ravished Psyche.

In a time of hypochondriacal philosophers
           children play happily in public gardens;
in a time of statistics
           anarchy denudes herself of the seventh veil;
and in a time of magistrates
           criminals invent new crimes;
in a time of hedonists and belly dancers
           wise men draw the blinds and bolt the doors.
In a time of journalists most decent things
           acquire the gift of invisibility;
in a time of death all of us suddenly
           and miraculously discover that we are alive.
Sometimes favour, if you will, the arrogant
           of intellect with an odour as of
unknowable roses, and the proud man
           with a pair of unreliable braces.
Upon autumn lakes scatter the feathers
           of foolish patriots in foreign fields,
and bring to the beds of those who suffer
           a benign sister with a handful of poppies

not for remembrance, but to forget.
        As to Arcadia also
I bring that overloaded old bag of the ego
        covered with coloured stickers
enumerating the travelogue of vanity and
        expensive guilt, to find
that forgotten poppy also
        growing among those mountains
that still hide the dithyrambical
        and deathless Pan.
But can I confide to you, mediator,
        the fear I fear I fear
faced with the sleight of hand you perform
        upon the ascending spheres and even
upon every day and the common place?
        As when rain chooses to fall upon
fields that need it, or the insane sun
        declines the whim to fry us like onions
or as the star-fished sea
        keeps to its beds and basins on
the classroom globe.
        These things can be seen, I know,
as subject to simple laws. And these are the mysteries
        I find myself facing with a kind of tremble.
For, as I see it, these natural laws
        comprise the only evidence I can perceive
of a superior purpose working
        up through all things. Thus when the old
tree falls in October wind (as no less
        the sparrow's feather) it falls because
it was ordained to fall not by the laws
        of Time or Newton, but by the will
that upon all things has imposed its natural
        and even supernatural purposes.
As in the recurring seven-veiled dance of
        physics and the conundrum

of prime numbers' *perpetuum mobile* or
       that diastole and systole at
the heart of things, the quixotic quanta, or
       the principle that seeks to teach us
a little intellectual humility,
       the will-o'-the-wisp perversity of
the hide-and-seek neutrino. It is then that
       though very darkly we might see
what your wish or your will may be:
       that, no less than
the madman killing or shark with a red jaw
       or the assassination of photographs or
the avalanche collapsing over
       Obermann villages or the entire
universe trying to find out
       how wide it is, so we obey your will
when we obey your image.
       And tremble, then, at the mystery of evil.
Let who will lay upon the stone
       of the run-over child a wreath
inscribed: *Dei voluntas*. I will not, for there is a mystery here
       not given to any, yet, to understand
The printed shadows of Hiroshima, do they
       point their evaporated hands at us
or you? How could it have been you?
       This is a thing so evil that
it could have come from nowhere save a mind
       capable of inventing the idea of evil.
We are, professor, out of joint with the purpose
       of your work; whatever that point may be,
we are out of joint with it. You know.
       Newman knew. We know. "The human race
is implicated in some aboriginal
       calamity." This is the mystery, this
calamity that, snakes coiled in its cloudy hair,
       sits on the great tripod of past, present

and what future, hypnotizing the dove
           with catastrophic images of the possible.
And so all the stories that little children play-act
           on their picnics or by winter firesides,
tales of the Polyphemi–Frankenstein monsters
           that waken up and eat us, this is what you
doctor have done. Here is the mad creature
           you have created. Have you built your own
murder into the marvellous faculties
           we use because we possess?
What does this shambling machine whisper
           as it crawls and stumbles among rocks and ruins,
its clockwork eyes clouded with self-hate, its
           terminals cancerous, wetware and wordwrite
alphanumeric, phonemed,
           automatic forks pick-
ing up isotopes, robotics utterly grouched,
           the reproductive generator hanging
down like an obsolete decoration, the
           anthropic spirit skinnered, the
enigma cybernized,
           the circuit of the nervous system worn
to a nexus of Freudian wires,
           what does this shambling machine whisper
when it encounters, down the dark path,
           halfway through a Black Forest, of
a midwinter midnight,
           the huge god riding on a dead white horse?
What, what does it whisper?
           "I am a man"?

Arbiter of dreams open my sleep-walking
           eye upon scenes I cannot recognize
when in the morning I wake among nightmares. Let me see
           some humane minds still uncorrupted, some

good men not angling for
        even bigger fishes and some
women not cultivating Chinese little fingernails
        and poisonous flower power,
some farmers not ashamed of the name George, some
        doctors prepared to prescribe for ailments
not amended by penicillin, some gardeners providing
        a herb we seem to have lost, the *herba sacra*;
some couples actually thinking of truly
        mutual pleasures; some children
playing games without guns and some priests
        practically praying. Some birds in nests
not for sale and at evening some edible browsers
        grazing at grass; some small kingdoms
not constructing sub-atomic megakills; some
        cities not gormandizing spaghetti junctions;
some gardens growing a little wild in
        southern seaside townships; some
African elephants in Africa;
        some sunrises to which we may awaken
without the mind clouded by those poisoned
        vapours that now hang over every
mushroom field. But "Complaint",
        said a holy man, "is sin." Those mists
of the morning slowly disperse as
        the light climbs higher; invalids eventually
throw off sheets and step out into
        everyday rituals; overgrown even
battlefields after a time. Through a window
        in the gutted mansion
a flowering bush sooner or later
        pushes its optimistic blossoms
and from haunted lives one day
        the ghouls have fled, leaving
the kitchen just habitable; in the waste land
        a gypsy family has set up a homestead,

and in the derelict heart a worm of hope
        is still found breathing under
a broken hearth stone. "All Nature, inasmuch as
        it is Nature, is good." For, somewhere,
hidden in its darkest heartland,
        down in the germinal and platonic
cave, dreaming in the sea, cradled in graves as
        sometimes glimpsed in clouds,
the origins of the possible speak to us
        of what we might do if
in this once heavenly setting we
        recollected fabled Arcadia
and why we lost it.

        At a time of conundrums and rabies
to inhale oxygen and to evoke
        supernatural precedents. At a time
of tubercular novelists and pot-bellied champions
        to sharpen pencils and rig up
large tents for boy scouts and chimpanzees.
        At a time of bad apples and short circuits
and popular comics to manufacture winter
        socks and encourage cricketers. At
a time of multiplying hysterics
        to collect tears and Jordan water.
Consecrate, master of ceremonies,
        the faithless mind to a faithful purpose
and turn the conscience of India towards
        social constructions superior to Taj Mahals
and the Christian missionary to
        a prettier position and the Mao Tse
Marxist to moments of fallibility and forgiveness.
        Allow dogs to survive in a world
from which they will undoubtedly soon be excluded
        and the whale to wallow about,

like us, for a little while longer.
                    To their domestic hearth let
all Argonauts return with their
                    cameras intact and a few sentimental
mementoes; pacify those who seek
                    to trouble fresh waters where the famished
hopelessly fish; load the wagons of harvest
                    gatherers with all sorts of fruit
including a real cornucopia; put down those
                    equine statues of field marshals who
mobilized, so they supposed, armies of digits; and
                    degrade all invigilators
because they trust no one; let
                    fall upon the Just some summer sunshine
as it does upon the Unjust; fend off
                    fire from the playing babe and attend,
dominie, those hundreds and thousands of us
                    who do not know the right thing to do.
Or is it all, really,
                    just for the birds? Then may we
learn a little from them. But consider, Paraclete,
                    the dove, devoted advocate of Venus,
anima, blandula, vagula,
                    that Picassoid pledger of peace,
does not this pure carnivore,
                    cave-mouthed like Chronos, devour
its own fledgling children
                    in the parsonage dovecote? Can
we appeal with any expectation of answers
                    to our local and more modest deities?
They are, after all, your higher executives,
                    branch managers, as it were, possessing
some administrative powers. What of
                    the jesus prayer or the curative
operations of oriental mantra?

32

What of the long history of
                small miracles at the Aesculapian
tabernacle? You, Jahweh,
                still, still asleep on Sinai? No,
they do not respond to these
                supplications addressed upward by
those whose devotion also dedicates itself
                to even dimmer demigods like money
or Lenin or the demon of
                social democracy or Liberty or
any of the other parthenogenical idols
                a cynical fancy flatters. These
deities sit around like
                museum plaster statues
allowing us all to cleanse their clay feet
                from vast lachrymatories
that copiously overflow now.
                And the little dog laughs to see such fun
and the fish runs away with the moon.

Illusions have spoken the truth in obscure language
                about matters we cannot speak of at all.
I mean the death of the heart
                that does not know it is dead because
it continues to suffer
                and like a headless chicken stalks around
bleeding Chinese ideograms signifying Pity
                down the garden path. As winter
fix the variable and valuable
                opinions of water, and the variant
mind that slips away down any
                conduit or convenience, fix it
with fortitude towards the purpose
                for which it must run up hill.

If certain colours of the spectrum
        and several notes of the diapason
remain beyond our perception
        why not several modes of existence
beyond our sublunary comprehension?
        We have yet to invent the instruments
capable of entering these spheres.

I have looked, as have so many others,
        in so many catacombs and hecatombs
that echo only with our futile footsteps,
        for you, the absconded. Who have gone
from all the places, gone from the grave and fountain,
        from the cave of the mind, gone from the shrine
and the forgotten shibboleth, gone from the fallen and
        shit-littered temple, the *pissoir* tabernacle,
gone from the infested altar and
        the screaming cathedrals,
left only cold air and the zero booming about us,
        gone from the heart where once
you surely broke bread in the human house
        without a sup of sorrow, gone from those
transfigured seas where an amoeba rose and
        monstrously prophesied revolution over
Darwinian waters—
        so many in so many clefts of the mind
seek even now. I have found nothing. Nothing.
        Not so little as on the rock
an Adam footprint, or the mind overturned
        to commemorate your passing.
Only, in the void an invisible
        alcove enshrining the huge sibyl
of your absence. Singing lamb, sweet Pascal,
        not the god of Abraham or Isaac,

not the god of philosophers and scholars,
          not even in the end the X one, but
whatever or whoever it is that
          we were invented to venerate.
Behind all the altars and the entablatured
          tabernacles, behind the mantra and the
unfolding mandelion, behind the mandala and the
          May *magnificat*, the *sanctum sanctum sanctorum*,
          beyond even the void, the *ideos* and the *logos*,
          behind all that can be spoken or imagined,
is it really there, the one thing
          we cannot ever know?

At a time of enigmas and pandoras,
          of treetop browsing questionmarks and labyrinths
where the faceless in wheelchairs regularly
          perform their daily round,
at a time of asking, knowing
          there are no even unsatisfactory answers,
at a time of hopeless appellations,
          to eavesdrop on the conversations of
canonical photographers, to memorize
          the regulations of suburban public gardens,
to calculate odd eclipses, and to operate
          mechanisms imposing order on the winds.
At a time of absolute silence
          to listen to its orations.

Come home, fisherman, come home, come home,
          leave the long-dead Aegean and old Arnold's
far colder sea to sleep without bad dreams
          wandering over the surface of this failure
of all faith, our truly dead sea. No flying fish now
flitter over philosophies, no dolphins dive
          down through the glooms of doubt to

find drowned mythologies; the blindfold sirens
        shriek only in hysterics, and
great argosies of ideas and archangels lie
        burning and broken and rolling
on the flim-flam rocks. And the heart—
        crying along the shores and years it runs
echoing again and ululating it
        mourns as it flies,
the suicidal lamentation of the god
        for the dying man.

Accord us, star of the sea, one ray like
        the X of a crime. Visit
the infant of strangled human innocence with
        a kiss of life out of
the flower's mouth.
        Star of the spirit delude us
with your beautiful hallucinations
        before we wholly believe
in our own futile illusions.
        At a time of terror and ecclesiastical
massacres to erect charitable
        institutions and schools
for penitential suicides. At a time of intolerance
        and the decimation of marsupials
to light candles in subversive
        chapels and to bury the dead
with tomahawks in their hands.
        At a time of coldblooded calculators
and rigorous bigots to plant
        druidical oaks and cultivate
impious Cagliostros. At a time of orations
        to listen to silences. Lead
homeward also the circuitous
        intellect wandering lost in the

arroyas of Arizona like a mad
		guilt-ridden somnambulist;
castigate the hypocritical atom; liberate
		from its liberties that chained
giant, noetic conscience. Let
		matter forgive Lord Rutherford
and light Albert Einstein. Militate
		against the military and
liquidate the liquidators. Upon all
		altruists in South America
allow an agape to shine, for
		in the aviaries of the spirit
all birds, even the decapitated,
		can sing, and in the green summer
of the compassionate mind
		the myxomatosized rabbit run wild
again and on the harps of gold Pythagoras
		even Mongolian children play
psychotic paeans and poems of praise.
		Among melancholy mansions blind
nightingales elect to regale us. Under polluted
		waterfalls where we have sat
paralysed by the loud laws of acquadynamics
		we have bathed tomorrow morning
under a sun of gentler dispensations,
		and from long-derelict underground junctions
departed on journeys to remote and mythological Jordans.
		Some of us have even been visited
as we knelt in silent shrines
		by charming criminals; to others of us
bunches of spring flowers
		sometimes appeared in autumn and
to others again from dirty dustbins
		the poetic phoenix like
a rocket arisen. For, ferociously
		apparelled in flayed human flesh,

indestructible ideals
                have walked among us, slinging
blood from Struwwelpeter's
                scissored fingers. Divers have
descended into Tuscaroras where
                our idols lie dumb-foundered and
brought dazzling up to us again
                marvellous images, more
memorable than mermaids, images
                marbled with memories
of moral vision,
                like dripping statues of
the heroic mythos.
                Where chance encounters
occurred between unfriendly
                children, there societies
of Miltonic birds have rhapsodized
                not only to commemorate
such occasions but also
                to teach us praise.
Sometimes these high-flying
                effigies have pursued us over
dark parks and vast ages
                and black waters, begging us
with broken voices never
                never to forget them. I have
sat down to breakfast with
                a lost cause and found that it
was neither lost, nor a cause.
                It was merely everyone
looking for everyone else to forgive us
                before we all die. Near the world's end
there is an old elm tree
                where this seemed sometimes to happen
but ten tons of Time fell
                out of a war and only

the shades remain. I lean my ear
        to the cellar wall
and hear the mad underground
        river roaring in flood
laden with killed chairs,
        corpses, the debris of graves,
dismembered limbs and memories
        that toss like the horns
of drowned cattle out of the floods
        and I know that I hear
the torrents of anno domini.
        This, then, is a scene
of many defeats by moonlight
        when every word was a deep
dishonourable wound and every
        act a betrayal and
every idea an evasion
        of what should but could
therefore never be done.
        I speak of this always
present war that none of
        the living ever survive
and of which the victor
        is always the ritual victim:
when, to vanquish the viper
        we begin to slither and coil,
or into the bully to beat
        battling bravadoes turn.
But how can any lines measure
        such immeasurably sad times
save in terms of blood-red
        revolutions of the heart
or of poppies that poison
        even our lachrymae christi?
The interior of this cathedral
        fills with a fear no candle

can seem to illuminate
          and no evening sunlight
a little tenderly relieve
          and no ceremonies sanctify
and no word speak for. This
          testament is constructed
out of old bones and discarded
          razor blades and
the stained-glass days of the dead.

As anarchy come among us
          when we sit studying the
hypocritical formalities of
          injustice in the Maze
as once in Kilmainham
          Macormack; as mercy
come among us
          when we ride holy cows
over those buried up to the neck
          in doubt or debt; as pity
come among us
          when we peruse newspapers,
the lives of the aged or
          those notes sung by
battered brides; as justice
          come among us if
we close our eyes upon
          Sten guns, millionaires' yachts or
the machinations of intemperate fanatics;
          as caritas come among us
when we cross the deserted
          Arabias between us all;
and as hope attend us when
          we stand on the high

diving-board over
>an empty future.
Between summer and autumn forbid
>an Ides of March to re-enter
as again between winter and spring;
>between intoxicated friends
disallow the fractionate rocks;
>between now and then introduce
one traumatic moment
>of mutual forgiveness;
between lovers discourage the growth
>of obscene hybrids, and between the
rogations of grief, water
>those lilies that dance. Conceal
from the cripple all instruments
>(such as the violin) shaped
like the bodies of demigods;
>show to the wild horse
the fate of the Otto cycle;
>hide in obscurities
our brilliant flashes of ignis fatuus or
>the putrescent intelligence;
reveal to those who truly forget themselves
>new vistas of
henceforth immaculate genealogies. Where decay
>kingdoms abandoned by kings
encourage the hegemony of
>that hardy perennial
the Athenian demon.
>Where the domestic cat
revives the luxors of
>pharaonic Egypt may
sphinxes with colossal queries
>trouble all feline dreams
of political power.
>Where houses of doubt and snow abound

arrange that a mild sun very faintly shines
                    every day. Let us cease to fear dust
and remember that even clay
                    feet walk around in a world
                    that every May Day restores.
                    At a time of fire-flecked dawns,
rancid milk bottles and outmoded medallions,
                    some slowly swimming martyrs bring
messages to those marooned
                    on unfamiliar foreshores. Allegories
arrive by electric trains daily, and,
                    met by meteorologists,
lug from their bags
                    documents attesting that they also started
from the Finland Station. And that also
                    they arrive armed.
At a time of reviewers, Chinese vulgarians and
                    methodical universes,
to speculate on the population of anthills,
                    to retire to the Turkish baths, and
to inflate Montgolfier balloons.

Teach us not to despair on Tuesdays
                    when all things seem to recede
into temporal mirrors, and
                    cover over with dust sheets
those effigies that ululate in the
                    abandoned mansions. Mark time
not with a red cross but a hyaline;
                    draw from the mad man's eye
the beam that blinds it and let
                    the dreams of Aphasia attend
those in mental institutions. Open over the soul's
                    appalling apertures

bridges like Saarinen wings
         and to those who are reduced to
the circumstantial lie
         allow a little latitude.

Let ghosts walk in Battersea Park
         without dreading an earthly encounter,
and rectify all the errors we make
in our golden account books. Allow
         us to sit down at open-air tables
without observing the dawn of
         the Dies Irae, or the clock
at last striking midnight. (Why do cupidons
         with gold wings loop garlands
in the air over those who dislike
         all children? Why do those
who love roses possess gangrened fingers,
         and why will the heroic salmon
never learn circumspection?
         What carpenter can construct
doors that open only to our good angel? What
         statesman listens to the dying sighs
of the white giants?)
         The snows of yesterday have returned
to those clouds from which they will fall
         tomorrow disguised as summer and
one day the seas will part and from the fissure
         Orpheus rise up festooned
with telephone wires to teach us
         the triumph of the incommunicable.
Why are heroism and devotion like
         great works of art? Because
they have no object beyond themselves?
         Why do poets stand around

43

like telegraph poles? Because
        all they can do is pass on messages?
At a time of bankers
        to exercise a little charity—

Elegy

This is not a requiem I make for them
where they lie under a stone or by a tree.
I make this to remember how I saw them
when, gabbing and hobnobbing, we
walked up and down a dirty world that looked
a little brighter through a glass of beer,
or, half seas over, stared up at the crooked
stars that are still just as crooked here.

But since there is nowhere for them to go to
outside that dirty world or further than
the faking zodiac with only moonshine to show to
the fugitive gulled ghost, then where can
they go save home here to the one
place where they know that, come what may,
here and hereafter they will not be alone
but hang around for ever and a day.

It does not matter who they are, the lazy
bones whom someone, somewhere, wishes
back into those hungover and sleazy
basements and bedrooms where they drank like fishes,
or those, loquacious with a glass in hand,
who brought Pegasus into the Black Horse bar
or a mermaid into Mooney's in the Strand.
It does not really matter who they are.

All of us have had such friends and such
intemperate or even temperate times.
To them, *dies non*, it does not matter much
when at eleven the clock at Mooney's chimes.
But when I hear the call, and then the bell
strikes the last time, and I get up to leave
the empty bar, I know perfectly well
I have met ghosts I do not disbelieve.

To you it does not matter who they are
the tartan shirted daubers and the shrill
lickspittle poets, always two drinks below par,
(or so they said) who swigged and blabbed until
what with the beery hubbub, the fag smoke,
the firework egos and the serpent tongues—
these ceremonies of memory evoke
times that resound down twenty years like gongs.

The lank Minton, always with too much cash,
lugging along a line of pretty boys
randy and rowdy, some filthy and some flash,
who made their mark according to their noise:
you paid the piper heaven knows what to play
a jig up, Johnny, but the dance of death
snaked through your life until that drunken day
when you, sad man, at last ran out of breath.

I think of Robert Colquhoun and Robert MacBryde
of that generation the two brightest guests
in spite of a few bad habits neither tried
either to make much of, or to hide.
I think of Marlais Thomas, who now rests
at last from blowing his own golden trumpet:
a man for whom the Muse, his life attests,
was a true wife and not a one-night strumpet.

And Randall Swingler, that most honest man,
sacrificing to the communist cause
everything he possessed, including an
inherent hate of bullying and wars.
Not to forget—I cannot—Brian Higgins
like a small bull let loose in a china shop,
and MacNeice, who knew that poetry begins
where the philosophical propositions stop.

And Archer, a David not cut in stone
but in the all too vulnerable flesh
of a man born to love, but live alone,
seeking the moral vision as the fish
follows its lethal fly. But the bait
always evaded him, and sank down the stream
leaving only a hook's wound to create
pain that only more pain could redeem

The sober Eliot, who saw two kinds of men:
those of us who know only too well
that what we are begs to be forgiven,
and those who cannot beg. In its cell
he watched, like a plain clothes police inspector,
the drunken human conscience rant and rave
and ravage Europe like the Marxist spectre
rising headless out of its own grave.

By a Welsh mountain with a few jamjar flowers
Tom Blackburn lies now, his haunted face
serene, I hope, at last, even at peace
after the big jump, after the cliffhung hours
that like a rock face he ascended until
there at the summit, in the christian air,
he clasped the sign that stood upon his hill:
"Cleave the wood, Tom, and I am there."

Where are they now? How can they be nowhere?
Can you rise from your grave? Their deaths stand here
like trees in the mysterious atmosphere
of evenings concealed, but we hear
the sussuration of leaves and the weird stir
of inexplicable wings and, transfixed, under
the lyres and tongues and leaves we stand and stare
upward into death, and into wonder.

They are all there now in my recollection,
golden-tongued, loudmouthed, alive, and dead.
Not a word they uttered, not an inflection
of those once glittering voices, or what they said
fails to evoke an echo or an answer
from a devotion deeper than memory lends.
And to these voices then, like an old dancer,
the heart arises and takes hands with friends.

The Ship of Fools

What happened to the ship of fools
    that sailed the winter sea
and to all the clever ones
    that sailed the ship with me?

When the lighthouse of the dark
    led on to a rock
that singing ship, did we sing on
    or did we die of shock?

And what about the sailormen?
    Are they all lying drowned
with questionmarks hooked in their jaws
    and the little fish all around?

With buttercups and daisies
    the little children played
and danced about under the stars
    completely unafraid.

The wise men in the moonlight
    strolled underneath the shrouds.
"Love," they said, "like moonshine, makes
    a halo in the clouds."

The heroes lolled about or sat
    combing their yellow hair
and picked their teeth and watched the red
    day dawn everywhere.

And to the wheel, like a fake saint
    the noble statesman bound
himself with lies and steered the ship
    sedately round and round.

Who were all the famous fools
        that sailed our pleasure cruiser
round the world and back again?
        And what was her name? *Medusa*?

The foolish virgins lay about
        the brimstone burnished decks
clasping Dutch caps in their hands
        and candles in their sex.

The millionaires sat counting
        their hard cash in the hold
and every penny of it fool's
        negotiable gold.

The lovers bucking on the bed
        groaned and kissed in pain
then slept awhile. When they awoke
        they set to it again.

The poor men pulled upon the ropes
        or sweated at the oar
because they knew that this is what
        they had been born for.

Down in the first-class stateroom
        there the Powers that Be
sat singing: "I'll love you if
        only you'll love me."

The priest stood priestifying at
        his little wooden ark.
"Beloved," he said, "God is not dead.
        He's whistling in the dark."

And through it all like a ghost through a wall
    strode the bold physicist:
"No matter, no matter," he chanted. "Matter
    simply does not exist."

Then winter befroze the crystal ship
    with icicles and snow
but like a wedding cake we sailed
    gaily into tomorrow.

The black birds flew around the mast
    like little bits of death
but everyone upon that ship
    just took another breath.

The Prince of Darkness came and leaned
    against the middle mast
and lo! our dreams like three great queans
    began to sashay past.

Hard, hard the hazard and the rock
    and bitter cold that sea.
But O with such a famous ship
    who so fine as we?

Did we hear the grinders roar
    or see the lightning flash
or feel the wind of heaven like
    a kamikaze crash?

No, all of us, yes, all of us
    simply went pursuing
our sweet dreams like three great queans:
    swilling and guzzling and screwing.

O long and late we boozed and ate
    and rogered at the game,
and if we had known what we know now
    it would have been the same.

What happened to the ship of fools
    that sailed the winter sea
and to all the clever ones
    that sailed the ship with me?